The RANGE ETERNAL

LOUISE ERDRICH

paintings by **Steve Johnson** and **Lou Fancher**

University of Minnesota Press | Minneapolis

First published in 2002 by Hyperion Books for Children

First University of Minnesota Press edition, 2020

Published by the University of Minnesota Press
111 Third Avenue South, Suite 290
Minneapolis, MN 55401-2520
http://www.upress.umn.edu

Original artwork prepared for printing by color specialist Timothy Meegan

LIBRARY OF CONGRESS CATALOGING-IN-PUBLICATION DATA
Erdrich, Louise, author. | Johnson, Steve, illustrator. | Fancher, Lou, illustrator.
The range eternal / Louise Erdrich ; paintings by Steve Johnson and Lou Fancher.
Minneapolis : University of Minnesota Press, 2020.
Identifiers: LCCN 2020022315 | ISBN 978-1-5179-1098-3 (hardcover)
Subjects: CYAC: Stoves—Fiction. | Family life—North Dakota—Fiction. | Ojibwa Indians—
   North Dakota—Fiction. | Indians of North America—North Dakota—Fiction. | North Dakota—
   History—20th century—Fiction.
Classification: LCC PZ7.E72554 Ran 2020 | DDC [E]—dc23
LC record available at https://lccn.loc.gov/2020022315

Printed in Canada on acid-free paper

The University of Minnesota is an equal-opportunity educator and employer.

26 25 24 23 22 21 20   10 9 8 7 6 5 4 3 2 1

To Aza
Migizi
Warm heart of our house!
—Mom

On cold winter days in the Turtle Mountains, I helped Mama cook soup on our woodstove, The Range Eternal. Bones went into the pot, for flavor, then potatoes and carrots. As I cut the onions, I held a kitchen match between my teeth. I still don't know why, but the match stopped my tears.

No two soups were ever the same. All were different. Right before we ate the soup, Mama took the bones out and gave them to grateful Rex.

Rex chewed his bones beside the stove, the warm heart of the house. After the soup, my brothers chopped wood and hauled it to the big, deep woodbox beside the door. Mama didn't think twice, later that evening, as she reached for a split log with one hand, stirred with the other, and kept the fire going.

When I came inside from doing my barn chores in the early dark, I stood by the mica window and watched flames dance. My cheeks went hot. My hands and feet thawed and prickled until they hurt, and finally, I stopped shivering.

THE RANGE ETERNAL was printed in raised lettering on the blue enamel of the door. I learned to write by tracing those letters in the air. I copied them down, with charcoal, in the margins of Daddy's newspaper. I tried to teach Rex, but he rolled away, comfortable in the heat, and began to snore.

At night, I pulled my cot away from the wall and slept facing the fire as it died down behind the glass. Mama wrapped a hot stone in wool and put it into my bed. I pressed my feet against its fading warmth.

When I was tucked into the stillness, I was sometimes afraid. Huge winds beat upon our walls. In the thick breath of storms, I heard the footsteps of Windigo, the ice monster. At the window, at the door, Windigo waited. Whenever my eyes closed, I was sure it drew near.

The stove was constant, saving me. The monster's snow fingers could not grasp through its heat. Those wind claws and ice teeth would melt away before I could be hurt. As the shadows pulled light across the ceilings and walls, I crept closer to the stove. Safe, I looked through its door into pictures of long ago.

I saw the range of the buffalo, who once covered the plains of North Dakota so thickly that they grazed from horizon to horizon.

I ran the deer range. I ran the bear range. I galloped the range of horses. I loped the wolf range and fox range, the range of badger. I flew the sky, the range of herons, of cranes, hawks, and eagles.

I saw The Range Eternal.

When I woke, the stove's heat was gone. Cold flowed in the blue air of the room. The breath of my sister in the rollaway was a feather standing above her lips. I curled fiercely into myself and waited as Daddy got up, ready for his day, in the next room.

When at last I heard the thump of boots going onto his feet, I knew it wasn't long before gray coals would blossom hot and red. Outside, Rex whined and hit the door with his front paws. He was no Windigo.

Daddy's shoulders rose over the stove as he fed strips of birchbark to the bottom of the firebox. He was no monster. He wouldn't melt.

The bark burst into light. I heard the kindling he added start to snap before he carefully placed two split logs on the hot flames and closed the door. Before he went outside, Daddy opened the stove vents all the way, and the logs caught fire. The roar of the heat was loud as wind, but warm. The night's fears seemed small.

It wouldn't take long for heat to flow around us. By the time we got out of bed, Mama was standing at the stove. With one hand she stirred the oatmeal smooth. The other sure hand reached for salt, sugar, sometimes raisins. My favorite jam was made from Juneberries dark with summer rain. As I stirred the sweet purple into my oatmeal, I was glad to think of hot days coming, when we wouldn't have to walk to school.

But Mama always had potatoes baking in the ashes. On those winter mornings, she gave them to us before we trudged deep snow trails over two hills, down a little back road. We walked the new range, the Turtle Mountain range, the range of woods and sloughs that we loved, and we were glad for the feel of those potatoes.

Heavy in our pockets, they kept our hands cozy, and later that morning, as we ate them, we tasted the warmth once more.

And then, one year, poles and wire went up along the road to our house.

Now we could touch a switch, and electric lights would pop on. Mama put away the wick lamps that burned kerosene. A new stove came down the winding road, chained onto the bed of a truck.

Now we could turn a knob and heat would flow through a coiled burner. We hauled the old stove out into the yard. A crow landed on the hood, pecked the shiny nickel trim. Our dog, Rex, sat for an hour in its shade. Onto the back of the same truck, Daddy and my big brothers and sister loaded The Range Eternal.

When the truck went down the road, the stove was still gleaming from Mama's polishing cloth. The fittings glittered in the sun, and the crow followed, curious, until at last the truck disappeared over the hill.

All summer, we were glad to have a stove that did not heat the entire house every time Mama made bread. But when winter came, we missed The Range Eternal. Even though we now had a little furnace to keep us warm, there were no hot flames, no ash-baked potatoes, no center to the kitchen, no warmed stones for my feet at night. Even under many blankets, I shivered, and Windigo came near.

Sometimes, in the freezing dark, I woke to feel its laughing breath. I had to tell myself that I was imagining too much. I had to close my heart over my fear. I breathed beneath my covers, put my hands across my ears, my eyes. I fell asleep, and as I slept, I got older.

I grew up.

I am a woman now, married, with my own job, a kitchen to come home to, and a stove where I can stand with my son, stirring soup in a pot.

All seems complete, yet there are times when I feel something missing. My son cries out in his dreams in the deep of night. The wind breaks against the windows. I long for a center of true warmth.

It was not until I passed the broad window of a store that sold old things that I knew what I missed. The Range Eternal. The Range Eternal.

Now I sit by the stove on cold winter afternoons. Sometimes, as the dusk lowers, I do not switch on the lights. I watch flames pull shadows down the walls. I teach my son to enter the pictures, the way I used to do.

Even here in the city, I show my husband and son how the animals race back and forth, across the walls to the horizon, beneath a deep and darkening sky. I keep the fire going. Together, we see again the old range, the vast range, the living range restored.

I keep The Range Eternal.

Author's Note

I have dim memories of this stove, The Range Eternal, from early visits to my grandparents' house on the Turtle Mountain Reservation in North Dakota. My mother always spoke of the stove (shown here in a painting by my sister Dr. Angela Erdrich) with such affection, and many times regretted that after all the warmth it gave, the old stove was lost. I have tried to return some of the old warmth to her in this book.